VANESSA AND VALERIE FLOURNOY

Celie and the Harvest Fiddler

PAINTINGS BY JAMES E. RANSOME

TAMBOURINE BOOKS NEW YORK

Text copyright © 1995 by Vanessa and Valerie Flournoy
Illustrations copyright © 1995 by James E. Ransome

Printed in the United States of America.
The text type is Goudy.
The illustrations were painted in oil on paper.

Library of Congress Cataloging in Publication Data
Flournoy, Vanessa.   Celie and the harvest fiddler / by
Vanessa and Valerie Flournoy ; illustrated by James E.
Ransome. — 1st ed.   p.   cm.   Summary: Celie, a young
African-American girl living in the South in the 1870's,
wants desperately to win the costume contest at the All
Hallows' Eve harvest festival. [1. Halloween—Fiction.
2. Masks—Fiction. 3. Afro-Americans—Fiction.] I.
Flournoy, Valerie. II. Ransome, James E., ill. III. Title.
PZ7.F66Ce 1995 [Fic]—dc20 94-47322 CIP AC
ISBN 0-688-11457-1.—ISBN 0-688-11458-X (lib. bdg.)

10 9 8 7 6 5 4 3 2 1
First edition

The autumn leaves swirled around Celie's feet as she raced down the forest path into town. Today the last of the summer crops had been harvested. All the root cellars and silos were filled to bursting.

The end of a bountiful harvest was always a time of celebration. But tonight would be extra special, for it was *All Hallows' Eve*. The time, it was said, when ghosts and spirits roamed the earth, and witches chanted into the night. But Celie wasn't afraid. The only spooky sounds she expected to hear were ghostly tales. The only spirits she expected to see were her neighbors

in their best costumes. Tonight, townsfolk and farmers alike would celebrate
All Hallows' Eve with a storytelling contest and a costume parade through
the town and neighboring countryside. If only Celie could win tonight's
prize for the scariest costume, her All Hallows' Eve would be perfect.

Celie's mind was so full of thoughts of the night to come, that she didn't notice her brother, Joshua, and his best friend, Zeke, until she nearly crashed into them.

"Hey, Celie!" Joshua shouted. "Watch where you're goin' girl!"

"Didn't mean no harm," Celie said, barely stopping, until she noticed their costumes. "What are you two supposed to be?"

"Can't you tell?" Joshua replied. "I'm a wild wolf boy. I've been roamin'
the woods all my life."

"And I'm a wild wolf boy too!" Zeke chimed in.

Celie smiled at her brother fondly. "Well, you don't look that scary to me,"
she said. "So outta my way. I gotta get ready."

Celie sprinted through the town square to the stable and climbed up into the hayloft. She pulled out a burlap bag where she'd hidden her costume. A few final stitches, and it would be ready.

From her high hiding place, Celie heard the rumbling of wagon wheels. Men were returning from market. The torches they carried cast a warm glow. It would soon be time for the parade to begin. People in and out of costume were already entering the town square. Some paraders slipped quietly out of the shadows. Others made noisier entrances. Celie couldn't wait to make her entrance too!

The last stitch was in place when Celie heard the faint sound of fiddling skipping on the wind. She changed into her costume and hurried down the hayloft ladder to join in the fun. Celie remembered the tales about a mysterious man who would appear at one celebration or another with his fiddle in hand. Whoops and hollers rose up from the crowd. Could it be him? Celie had always thought the stories about the Fiddler were make believe. But here he was!

The Fiddler struck up another tune just as Celie squeezed through the crowd and entered the square, hoping to frighten everyone with her scary costume and a wild dance. With arms flung wide she pranced and leapt into the air, then whirled about in one final mad spin.

The Fiddler's spritely tune could barely be heard. But there were no

gasps or screams of fright. Everyone was laughing. Laughing at her! Joshua and Zeke were laughing the loudest.

Looking down at herself, Celie sadly saw why. Most of her wonderful costume lay on the ground around her. This wasn't what she wanted at all. Celie ran as fast as she could.

She ran past the crowd, into the forest, and down a sloping hill until she
came upon a flowing brook. In the brilliant moonlight, Celie looked into the
water and saw herself as everyone else did. Her costume had fallen apart.
She simply couldn't go back to the parade looking like this.

How long Celie sat she didn't know. Then she heard it. The sound of
a fiddle. Celie spun around, and sitting on a log right behind her was the
Fiddler.

Celie was certain she had heard the Fiddler's music. But she saw neither fiddle nor bow.

"Wasn't right for everyone to laugh at you. I bet you worked hard on that costume." The Fiddler smiled. "But the night's still young. You can catch up with the parade when it heads back to town."

"But my costume is ruined," Celie sighed. The Fiddler gave Celie a wink, and a colorful striped bag appeared out of nowhere.

"This here bag's been in my family for many a year. It's made of special cloth from my parents' parents' village far away across the sea. It's held a surprise or two. Perhaps it holds something special for you this night. Now make a wish."

Celie's wish was easy—a costume good enough to win top prize.

From inside the Fiddler's bag Celie pulled the most unusual mask she'd ever seen. As the clouds passed over the moon, the face on the mask appeared to change. Celie's eyes grew wide with wonder. The mask looked like it was alive!

"Now just remember, this mask isn't for anyone but you," the Fiddler warned. "So be careful with it."

Celie didn't understand.

"Don't worry, Celie girl," the Fiddler added. "Just enjoy tonight. I promise this'll be one All Hallows' Eve you'll never forget."

The mask fit perfectly and felt lighter then air. In the distance she heard the laughter of the paraders and music from a fiddle. That couldn't be. Yet when Celie turned around to thank the mysterious man, he was gone.

"That Fiddler sure can move fast," Celie said. But he was right, she had plenty of time.

Celie had nearly caught up with the parade. It was just reentering town when she noticed Zeke and Joshua straggling behind along the wayside. "Some wild wolf boys you two are!" she yelled as she overtook them.

"That's right, Celie girl," Joshua said, recognizing his sister's voice. "We're

the scariest, wildest wolves...." Joshua didn't finish his sentence. "Is that really you, Celie?" he sputtered. "Where'd you get that mask? Let me see it."

"Me too!" said Zeke.

Both boys grabbed the mask and nearly had it off Celie's head before she pulled away.

"Oh, no, you don't," Celie said. "This here mask is mine, and I'm gonna win the prize." Wasting no more time on her brother and his friend, Celie hurried to town.

The final judging of the costumes was about to begin when Celie entered the town square. This time her entrance was greeted with whispers of excitement from the crowd as she whirled and danced to the Fiddler's tune. Louder and faster, faster and louder, the Fiddler played until Celie collapsed in the middle of the square. Then the applause began. Celie couldn't wait to show everyone who was under the mask, when she heard Joshua call out, I *still* want to try that mask on for myself."

"Me too," said Zeke.

Celie turned to her brother's voice, but she couldn't believe her eyes. Coming toward her weren't two boys but two little wolves.

"Well what you starin' at?" said a wolf with Joshua's voice.

Suddenly Celie understood the Fiddler's warning. Joshua and Zeke had

wanted to be wild wolf boys. When they touched the mask, the boys *almost* had their wish come true.

"Mister Fiddler. Mister Fiddler. How do we put things right?" With a pluck of his bow, the Fiddler was at her side.

"Back to the brook quickly," he whispered.

Celie ran out of town with the wolves nipping closely at her heels, pleading to try on the mask. But when clouds blocked the moon's bright light, Celie lost her way. She finally tumbled down the hillside and rolled to a stop near the the brook's edge.

Celie sat up and looked about. The mask was gone. The wolves were gone too.

A faint melody filled the air, and once more the Fiddler was at Celie's side. He helped Celie up and sat her on a nearby rock.

"Well, did your wish come true?" the Fiddler asked.

Celie nodded and smiled. "I *know* the mask was the best costume anyone wore tonight. For that, I thank you. But I'm worried about Joshua and Zeke. Where are they, Mr. Fiddler? And, what happened to the mask?"

The Fiddler touched his nose with the bow of his fiddle. He reached inside his bag and pulled out the mask. Its eyes were now closed as if in sleep. Then the Fiddler played a sleepy tune, and out of the bushes crawled Joshua and Zeke.

"Look, they're back, Mr. Fiddler. Thank you!" shouted Celie.

"Whatcha mean *we're* back?" said Joshua. "We was just restin'. All that walkin' made us tired."

"And who are you talkin' to out here anyway?" Zeke yawned.

Celie turned about. "Why him silly, I'm thankin' Mr.—" But the Fiddler was gone!

Mama and Papa greeted the three children when they entered the town. They told them how the Fiddler had vanished, and how the winner of the costume parade had been chased out of town by two wolves. Now the top prize couldn't be awarded. No one knew who had worn the mask.

Joshua and Zeke couldn't believe the excitement they missed. They

promised to remember next year to take a nap *before* the parade got underway.

Celie listened and smiled. She thought of the Fiddler, his magical striped bag, and the mask. Her costume had been the best. But although she couldn't collect her prize, Celie didn't care. She'd not only gotten her wish but much more—a special tale to tell next All Hallows' Eve.

A jaunty melody drifted on the night's breeze. The Fiddler had been right.
This had been one All Hallows' Eve Celie would never ever forget!

E
FLO

5/96